Based on the fairy tale by E.T.A. Hoffmann

First published in Belgium and Holland by Clavis Uitgeverij, Hasselt – Amsterdam, 2014
Copyright © 2014, Clavis Uitgeverij

English translation from the Dutch by Clavis Publishing Inc. New York
Copyright © 2015 for the English language edition: Clavis Publishing Inc. New York

Visit us on the web at www.clavisbooks.com

The Nutcracker written and illustrated by An Leysen
Original title: *De Notenkraker*
Translated from the Dutch by Clavis Publishing

ISBN 978-1-60537-236-5

This book was printed in August 2015 at Proost Industries NV, Everdongenlaan 23, 2300 Turnhout, Belgium

First Edition
10 9 8 7 6 5 4 3 2 1

The NUTCRACKER

An Leysen

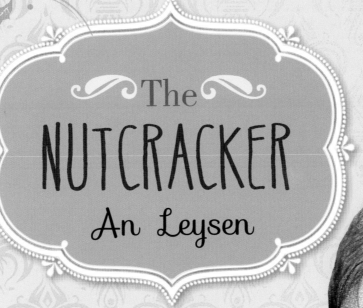

Clavis

NEW YORK

It is Christmas Eve. CLARA sits by the window and looks dreamily
at the snowflakes falling softly onto the vast carpet of snow outside.
Downstairs the adults are busy preparing for the Christmas party.
Clara is very curious, but Mom told her that she and her brother Fritz
can only come down when everything is ready.

IN THE KITCHEN the goose is already in the oven. Cookies in the shape of stars, angels, and small Christmas trees have been decorated with sugar frosting. Big bowls with vegetables and sauces are on the kitchen table. It all smells so delicious….

Clara and Fritz can't wait to taste all those yummy things. They tiptoe down the stairs and try to catch a glimpse of the Christmas tree through an open door.

THE TREE IS HUGE! It looks even bigger than last year's tree and is beautifully decorated. Shiny decorations hang from the branches: golden garlands, candy canes, and all sorts of figurines. But Clara and Fritz are only interested in what lies underneath the tree – the presents. Clara sees a doll in a cute pink dress, a doll's baby carriage, and a little umbrella. The big toy train and the military suit with the wooden sword are almost certainly for Fritz. Around those toys there are more surprises and heaps of candy.

CLARA AND FRITZ are so excited they forget they aren't supposed to be downstairs yet. They burst into the room. **"Little rascals!"** Mommy scolds. She tries to look stern, but when she sees the children's happy faces, she can't hide her smile.

THEN THE DOORBELL RINGS.

"Uncle Drosselmeier!" Clara and Fritz call together. Uncle Drosselmeier isn't their real uncle; he's a good friend of their father's. He looks a bit funny with his wrinkled face, but his eyes seem to have little lights dancing in them. He is wearing a festive outfit in bright colors and has a wig with big white curls on his almost bald head.

Clara and Fritz love him. Uncle Drosselmeier not only tells the best stories, he is also a very good craftsman. Every Christmas he brings the children a special gift that he made himself. This year he gives them a castle with turrets and flags. There are small puppets behind the windows. When Clara turns the key, the music starts to play and the puppets start to dance. They dance the same little dance to the same tune. Clara loves it, but Fritz soon gets bored. He'd rather have something he can actually play with. He thinks that the army of tin soldiers Uncle Drosselmeier chose especially for him is much more exciting.

CLARA gets a kind of soldier too, but one with a big head and a row of enormous teeth. "It is not just a soldier," Uncle Drosselmeier says. **"You can crack real nuts with his teeth! Go on, try it!"** Fritz thinks the nutcracker looks silly, but Clara loves his big, kind eyes.

Clara takes THE NUTCRACKER into her arms and lets him crack nuts for her. She looks for the smallest ones, so her little friend doesn't have to open his mouth too wide. Fritz wants to try it too, but he isn't as careful as his sister and he shoves the biggest and hardest nut he can find between the soldier's teeth. **CRAAACK!** An ominous crunch sounds, and the nutcracker's three front teeth break off. Now he looks even sillier.

"Look what you did!"

Clara has tears in her eyes. For a moment it looks as if the nutcracker's eyes look sad too. **"Don't worry,"** Uncle Drosselmeier tells her, **"I'll fix him tomorrow. Tonight is for celebrating!"** Clara doesn't feel like celebrating at all. She is glad when the evening is finally over and all the guests go home. Very carefully, so she doesn't hurt him, she carries the nutcracker to her room and puts him beside her bed.

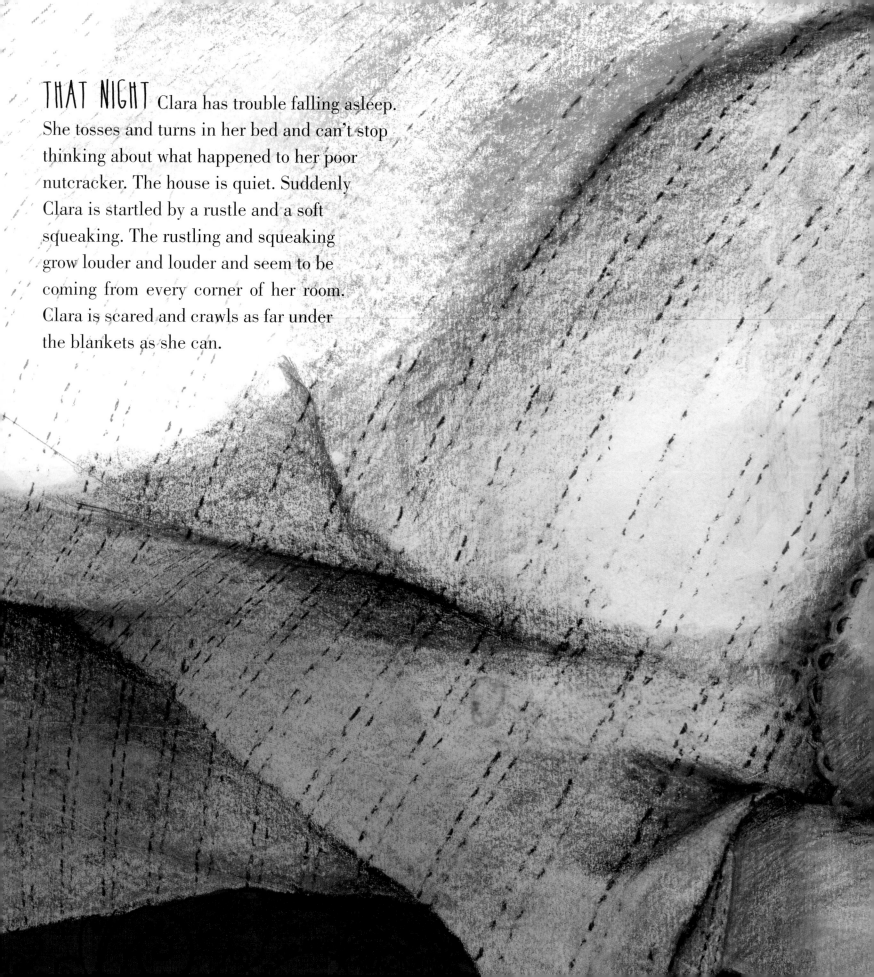

THAT NIGHT Clara has trouble falling asleep. She tosses and turns in her bed and can't stop thinking about what happened to her poor nutcracker. The house is quiet. Suddenly Clara is startled by a rustle and a soft squeaking. The rustling and squeaking grow louder and louder and seem to be coming from every corner of her room. Clara is scared and crawls as far under the blankets as she can.

THEN SOMETHING MAGICAL HAPPENS.

A sudden flash lights up the room, and everything around Clara seems to be spinning. She feels herself shrinking until she is the same size as one of her dolls. Now Clara can see where all that squeaking and rustling is coming from. A huge army of mice is marching through her room, led by their king. The mouse king has nasty little eyes, sharp dangerous looking teeth, and a big golden crown on his head. He looks terribly scary. Clara looks around, frightened. She is surrounded by the army of mice.

She has nowhere to go!

"ATTACK!" calls a loud voice behind Clara.
It is the nutcracker.
His broken teeth are whole again and
Clara's dolls and toys are behind him,
along with Fritz's army of tin soldiers.
Even the toy train is there. Before Clara
realizes what's going on, the mice and the
army of toys start to fight. Clara's dolls put
up a good fight, but they are no match for the
mean mice. Soon it looks like the toy army
will lose the battle.

Clara has to do something! As fast as she can, she runs
to Fritz's room to look for his wooden sword. She sees
the nutcracker standing face to face with the terrifying mouse
king, and with all her strength she throws the sword.

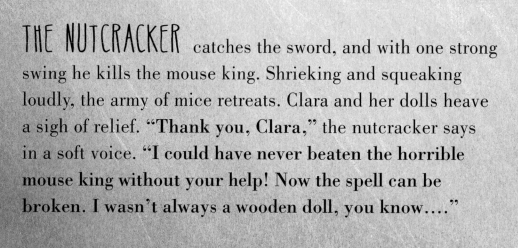

THE NUTCRACKER catches the sword, and with one strong swing he kills the mouse king. Shrieking and squeaking loudly, the army of mice retreats. Clara and her dolls heave a sigh of relief. "Thank you, Clara," the nutcracker says in a soft voice. "I could have never beaten the horrible mouse king without your help! Now the spell can be broken. I wasn't always a wooden doll, you know…."

And then he tells the incredible story of how he became a nutcracker.

ONCE UPON A TIME there was a king who loved parties.

He often invited his friends to the palace. The queen made her famous pies.
One day, when the queen was preparing another festive dinner, she heard the soft
pattering of mouse paws. It was the mouse queen, who lived with her mouse family
in the basement, and every now and then she would come up to get a snack.

"Let me taste," she begged in a high, squeaky voice.
"I am a queen too and I want to try it."

The queen was in a good mood and gave the little mouse a few tender pieces of meat.
The mouse queen loved it. She grabbed one piece after another with her small
mouse paws and ate with great relish. But then the mouse queen's uncles
and aunts and cousins and nieces appeared, followed by her seven
rude mouse sons. They jumped into all the pots and pans in the royal
kitchen... and soon there was nothing left of the festive meal except
for a few scraps of bread.

Her cheeks red with shame, the queen had to tell her husband
the party was cancelled because there wasn't anything to eat. When
the king heard what happened, he got so angry he ordered that the
castle be filled with mousetraps.

Soon all mice in the castle were caught, except for the mouse
queen; she was far too smart to get caught in a trap. She was furious
when she found out her beloved mouse family had been caught and
tossed out of the palace.

"You will all pay for this!" she squealed. "Just you wait!
When you have a child, the whole mouse family
and I will take revenge."

The king laughed away the threat, but when their
daughter was born a few years later, the queen
took the necessary precautions.

THE LITTLE PRINCESS was called Pierlepat and slept in a huge bed. There were at least twenty cats on the bed. They were there to make sure no mice could reach the girl. At first the cats kept a close eye on her, but after a while they fell asleep or started playing games with one another.

And that's how, one night, the mouse queen was able to take revenge. She climbed onto the bed and bit the poor princess in her face.

The princess's pretty face changed: her mouth grew huge, she had big sharp teeth, and her sweet smile became a terrible grin.

THE PRINCESS grew up and her mouth grew bigger every day. Her behavior became stranger too. She ate only nuts, which she cracked with her razor-sharp teeth, and every time she caught a glimpse of her own reflection in the mirror, she ran through the palace, screaming with horror.

THE KING AND QUEEN loved their
daughter very much, even though she
didn't look like a princess anymore and even
though the only thing she did was crack
nuts. They invited doctors and professors
from all over the country to cure her, but
nobody came up with a solution.

One day a little old lady arrived at the
palace. She predicted the princess would
only become herself again if a young man
cracked the hardest nut in the country,
and then handed it to her without being
startled by her face. But the old little lady
warned them too: if the princess did not
love the young man back, he would be
the next victim of the spell.

The king promised his whole kingdom to
the prince who could break the spell —
because of course he hoped his daughter would be saved by a prince. Princes
from far and near came to the palace,
but either they broke their teeth on
the nut, or they were so shocked by
the princess's face that they ran away.

Soon all THE PRINCES had tried their luck. Alas! Princess Pierlepat still looked repulsive. The king and queen were at their wits' end.

One day a soldier came to the palace. Although he was a simple soldier, he was exceptionally brave. He had strong teeth and had never been scared by anything in his whole life. He wasn't frightened by the princess's enormous mouth and her razor-sharp teeth, and he desperately wanted to win her heart. He cracked the nut without blinking and chivalrously presented it to the princess.

The old woman's prediction came true. When the princess took the nut from the soldier, the mouse queen's spell was broken and her horrible grimace changed into a beautiful smile.

But then something happened that no one had expected. The princess didn't see how brave and handsome the soldier was. Instead of thanking him, she started to cry.

"Father, Mother," she sobbed, "I don't want to marry a simple soldier! I am a princess and I only want to marry a real prince!"

As soon as she had finished saying the words, the soldier's mouth grew bigger and he changed into a wooden doll.

"And that's how," the nutcracker ends his story, "I became a nutcracker. And I would have been doomed to fight those ugly mice forever if you hadn't helped me."

"COME ON, CLARA. Now that the horrible mouse king is dead, I can show you where I come from." The nutcracker takes Clara by the hand, and suddenly they are no longer in her bedroom. They are in the middle of a lake, in a golden boat pulled by two dolphins. Clara can't believe her eyes. When she looks over the edge of the boat into the water, she thinks for a moment that she sees Princess Pierlepat's face in the water.

"Princess Pierlepat must be
the prettiest princess alive,"
Clara sighs dreamily.

The nutcracker laughs.
"That isn't Pierlepat you see
in the water, Clara.
It's your own reflection!"

CLARA ENJOYS THE BOAT RIDE. They pass at least twenty small villages, which all look strange. The houses look like toy houses, and candy grows on the trees instead of fruit. And everywhere they go, people wave at them with big smiles on their faces. It all looks like one big party.

"We are here!" the nutcracker says proudly when a huge palace appears from out of the mist. The turrets are beautifully decorated with colorful flags. It looks a little like the castle Uncle Drosselmeier gave them as a Christmas gift, but it's as if the palace is floating on the clouds.

The nutcracker jumps out of the little boat before they even get to the bank. "Hurry, Clara. The Sugar Plum Fairy is waiting for us!"

WHEN THEY REACH THE PALACE GATES, Clara hears
music. The music sounds so cheerful that Clara can't help herself.
She does a few dance steps, and then pretty ballerinas surround her.
They wave at Clara and the nutcracker to follow them.

"These are the Sugar Plum Fairy's maids of honor,"
says the nutcracker. "They dance all day long. Unfortunately
they only know one dance, and they repeat it over and over
again," he adds apologetically. But Clara doesn't mind at all.
She can't imagine she would ever get tired of the dance or the music.

CLARA AND THE NUTCRACKER follow the ballerinas
through a maze of chambers and hallways until they reach
a big hall. In the middle of the hall there is a beautiful lady
on a beautifully decorated throne.

"The Sugar Plum Fairy," the nutcracker whispers to Clara.

"Clara," the Sugar Plum Fairy says, her voice clear as a bell.
"You are a very brave girl. With your help, my friend the nutcracker
was able to defeat the mouse king and his dreadful army. Now that the mice
have disappeared forever, I can finally break the mouse queen's spell."

THE SUGAR PLUM FAIRY CLAPS HER HANDS THREE TIMES.

A wonderful light fills the room and almost blinds Clara. Everything around her
is lit by blue and pink, like a beautiful winter sunset.
Suddenly a handsome young soldier is standing next to her.

"You saved me, Clara," the soldier says softly,
and Clara immediately recognizes the nutcracker's voice.

"You are so different from Princess Pierlepat.
She couldn't love a simple soldier, but you cared about me,
even though I was just a silly wooden doll. I will never forget that."

THE SOLDIER SMILES at Clara and then walks up to the
Sugar Plum Fairy. He bows before her, kisses her hand, and asks
her to dance with him. The music starts up again, magical and
beautiful. Clara watches her brave, kind friend dancing with
the Sugar Plum Fairy. They seem to float through the hall,
and everything around them starts to glow. Then the ballerinas
join in and start dancing too. It is all breathtakingly beautiful.
Clara can't remember the last time she was so happy.
But the music starts to fade and Clara feels her eyes get heavy.

So very heavy it is impossible to keep them open….

IT IS CHRISTMAS DAY.

Clara is woken by a thumping sound that seems to come from the kitchen. She looks around her. She is no longer in the Sugar Plum Fairy's castle; she is back in her own bed. And she is just as tall as she was before. Was it all a dream?

Then Clara sees the nutcracker at the foot of her bed.

It's strange, his teeth are no longer broken, and for a second he seems to be smiling at her.

DOWNSTAIRS FRITZ IS PLAYING
with his tin soldiers near the Christmas
tree.
"How strange," he mumbles when he sees
Clara. "Yesterday they were all new and
shiny, but now it looks as if they've been
in a battle. Do you know what
happened?" Clara tells Fritz the whole
story about the fight with the mouse king and
Princess Pierlepat and the Sugar Plum Fairy.
Fritz looks at her and laughs.

"It was just a dream!" he says.

But Clara knows what she saw. She hugs
the nutcracker tight and wishes that from
now on every Christmas Eve will be as
magical as this one.